All I Did

written by Lucy Floyd
illustrated by Marc Mongeau

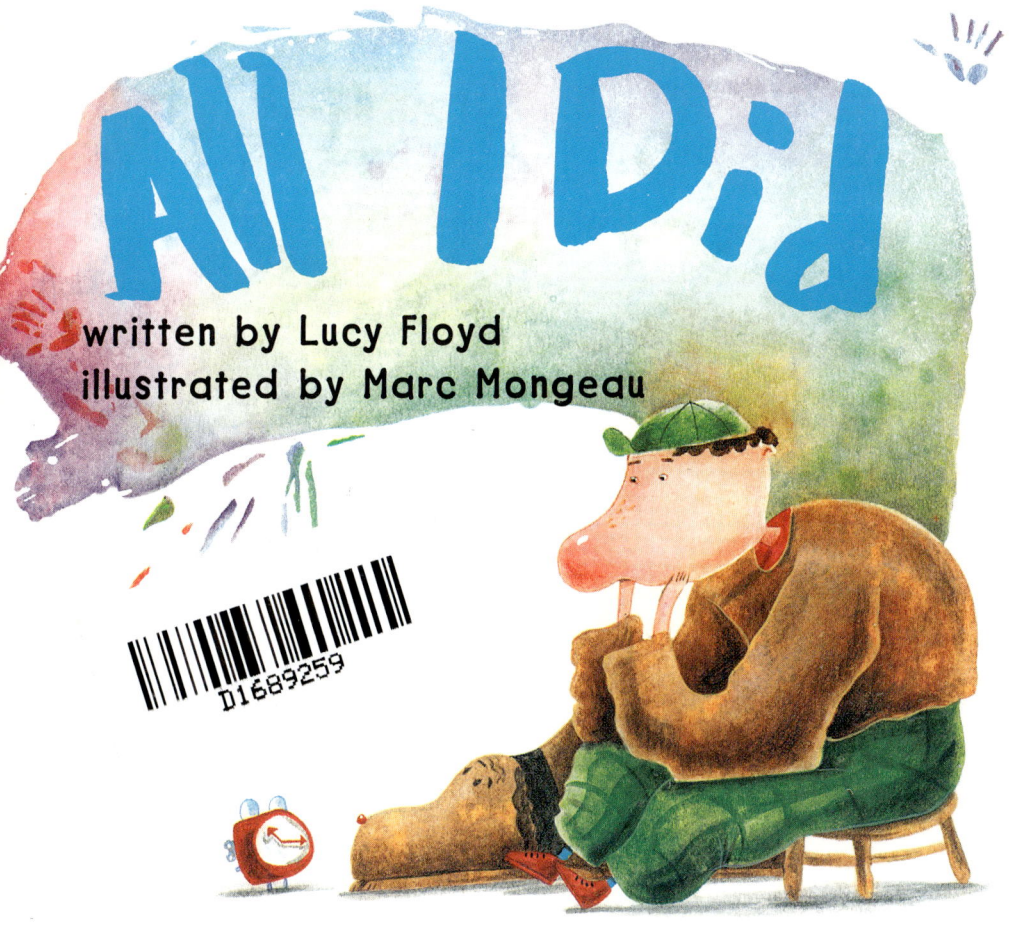

HARCOURT BRACE & COMPANY

Orlando Atlanta Austin Boston San Francisco Chicago Dallas New York
Toronto London

All I did was run in the house and Mom said,
"Time out."

All I did was fix up my room and Mom said,
"Time out."

All I did was hop on the table and Mom said,
"Time out."

All I did was clean up the rug and Mom said,
"Time out."

All I did was eat lots of cake and Mom said,
"Time out."

"I have too much time out,"
I said to Mom.